# Rat and Jam

By G. Wilkinson
All Rights Reserved. © Copyright G. Wilkinson 2018

Disclaimer:
No part of this book may be reproduced or transmitted in any form or by any means, mechanical or electronic, including photocopying or recording, or by an information storage and retrieval system, or transmitted by e-mail without permission in writing from the publisher.

# Reading Sprouts:

Reading Sprouts books are graded readers designed to support first-time readers taking their first steps into reading. They begin with short simple sentences and three letter phonic words only. Each story is short to avoid overwhelming children with too much text in the beginning and are accompanied with bright funny pictures to spur a child's interest in reading, Reading Sprouts' aim is to support first-time readers, build their confidence, and encourage reading enjoyment.

At the back of every story there is a story guide for parents and children. Each story guide ellicits questions parents can ask their children about the story to check reading comprehension and promote further thought and discussion about the characters, morals in the stories, and how the story is relatable to them.

To my wife, Atsuko, thank you for your love, support, and infinite patience.

Rat and Jam

Rat has jam.

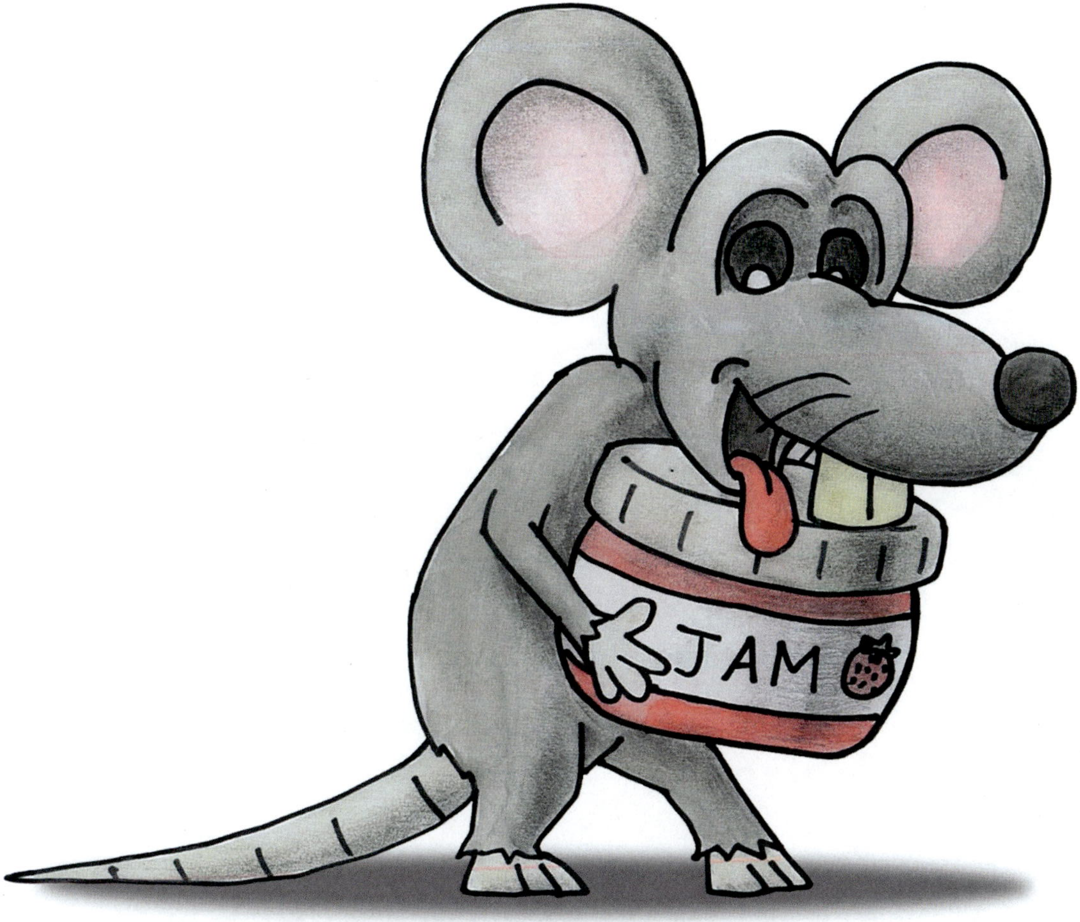
JAM

Bat taps Rat.

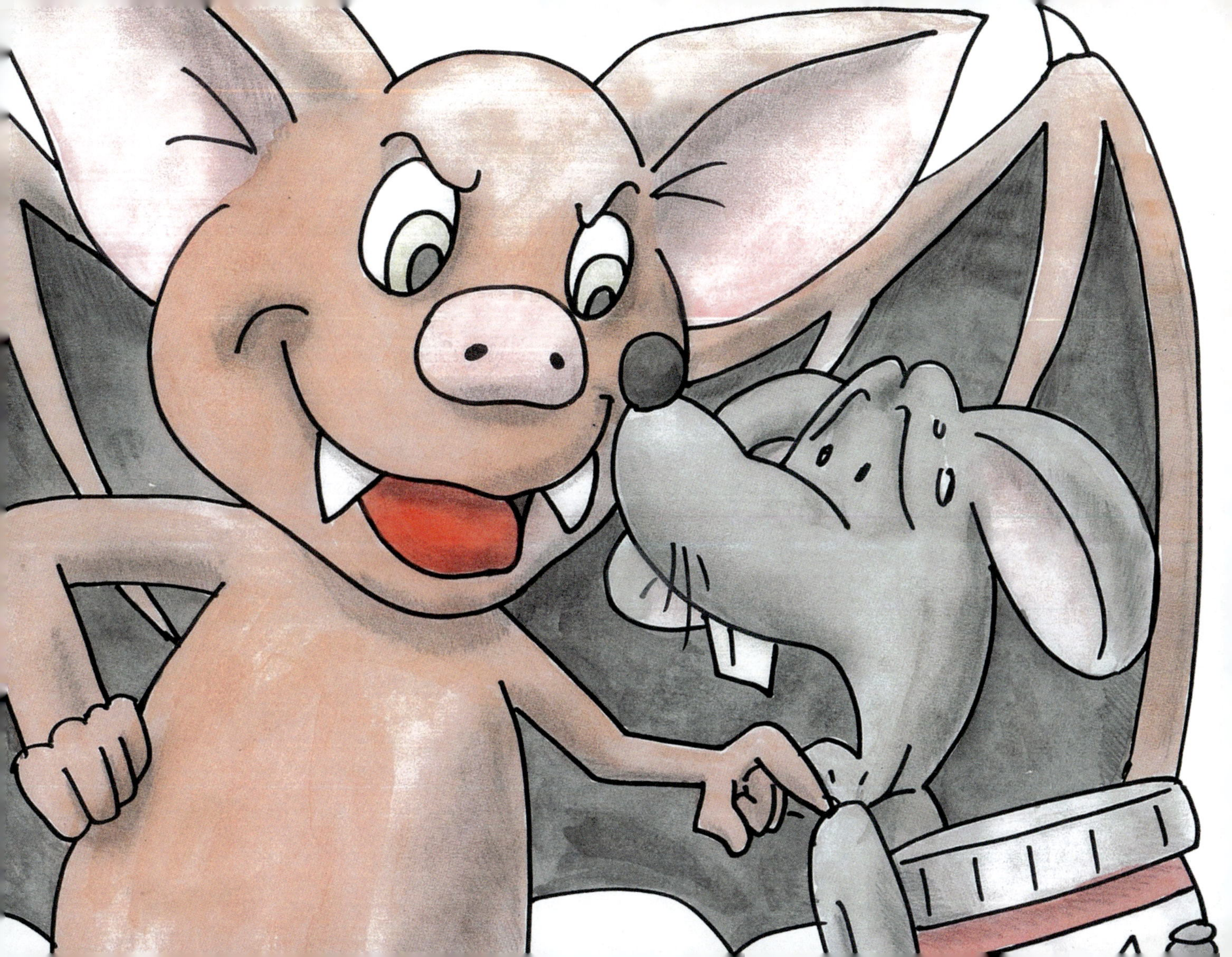

Bat has jam.

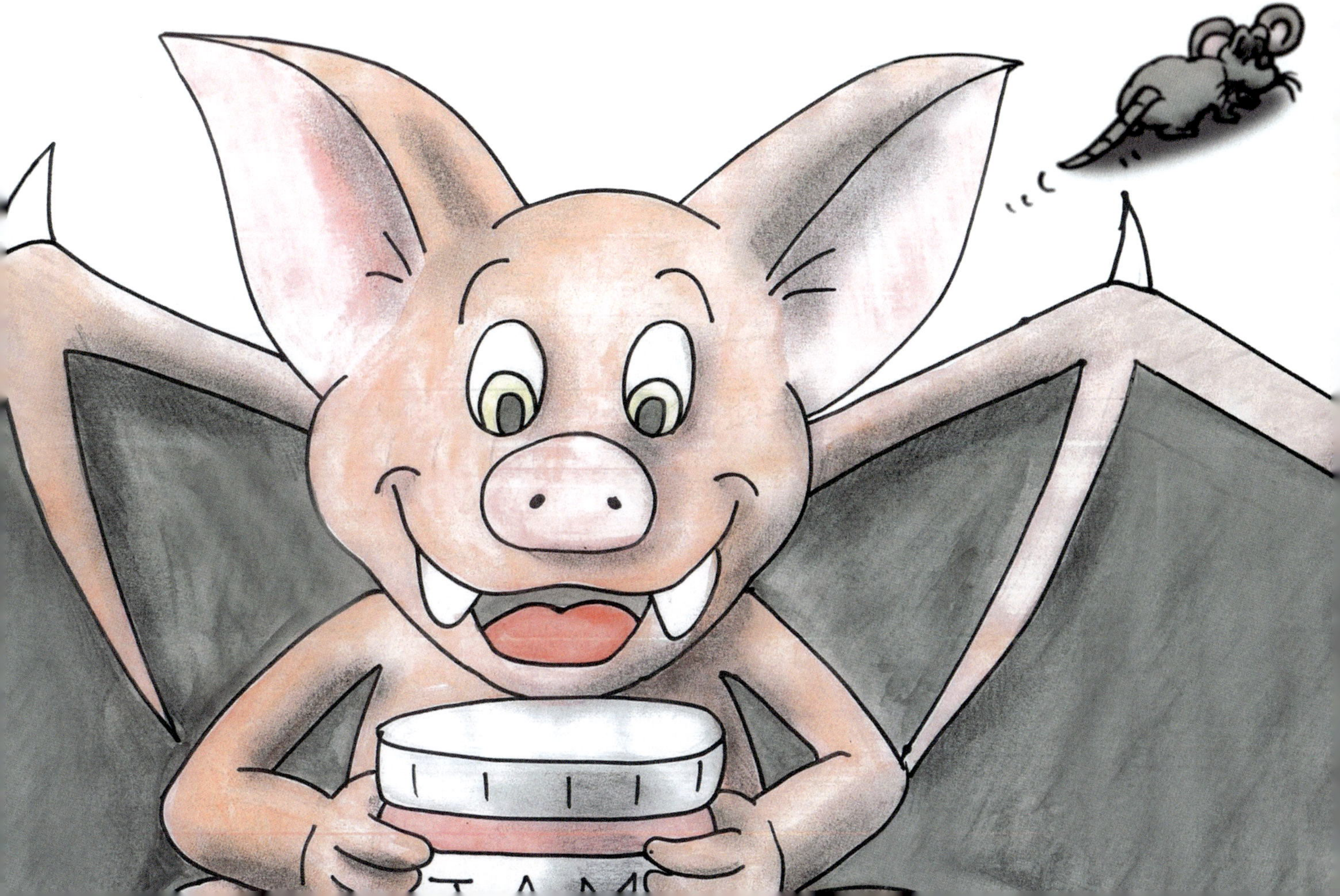

Cat taps Bat.

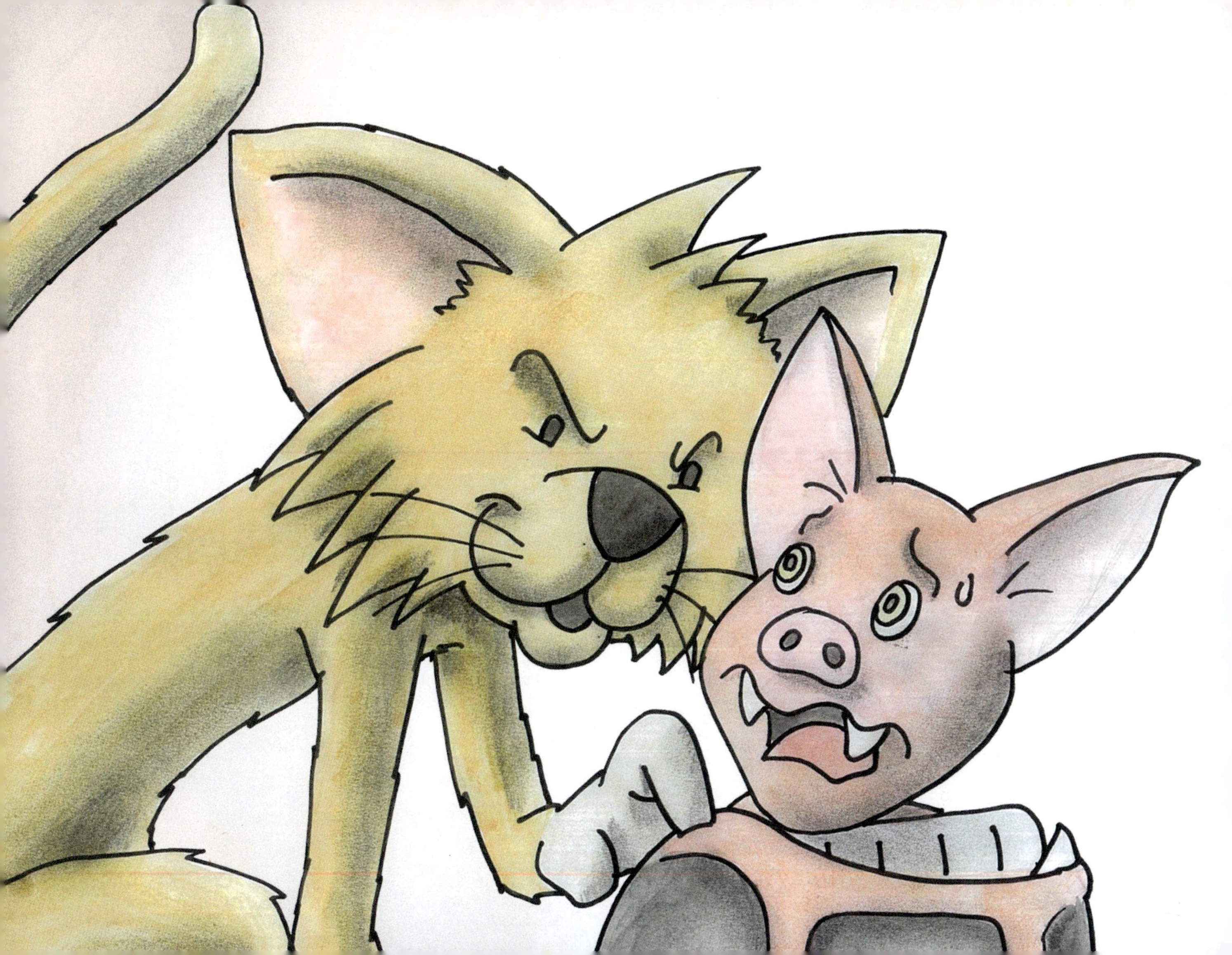

Cat has jam.

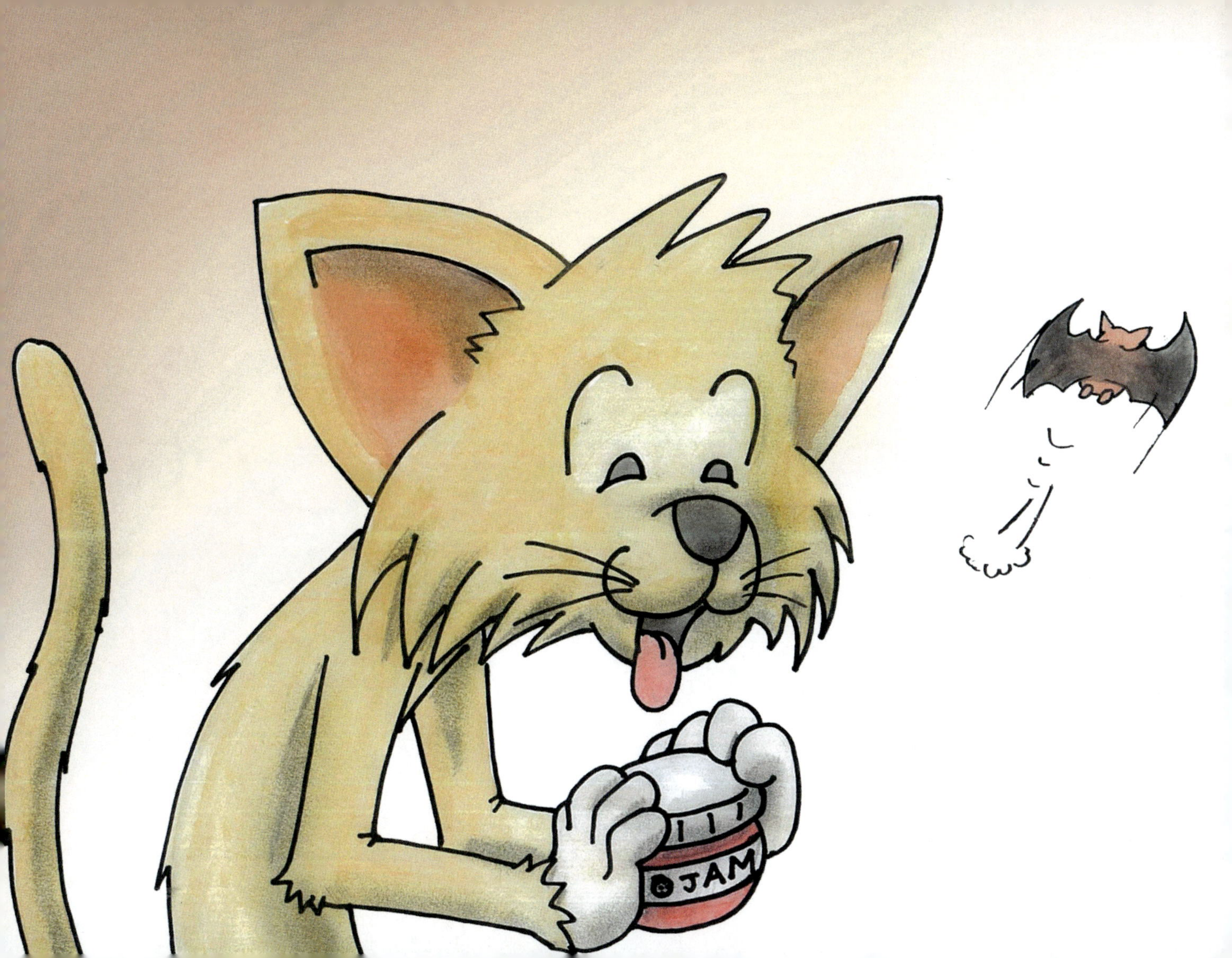
JAM

Dog taps Cat.

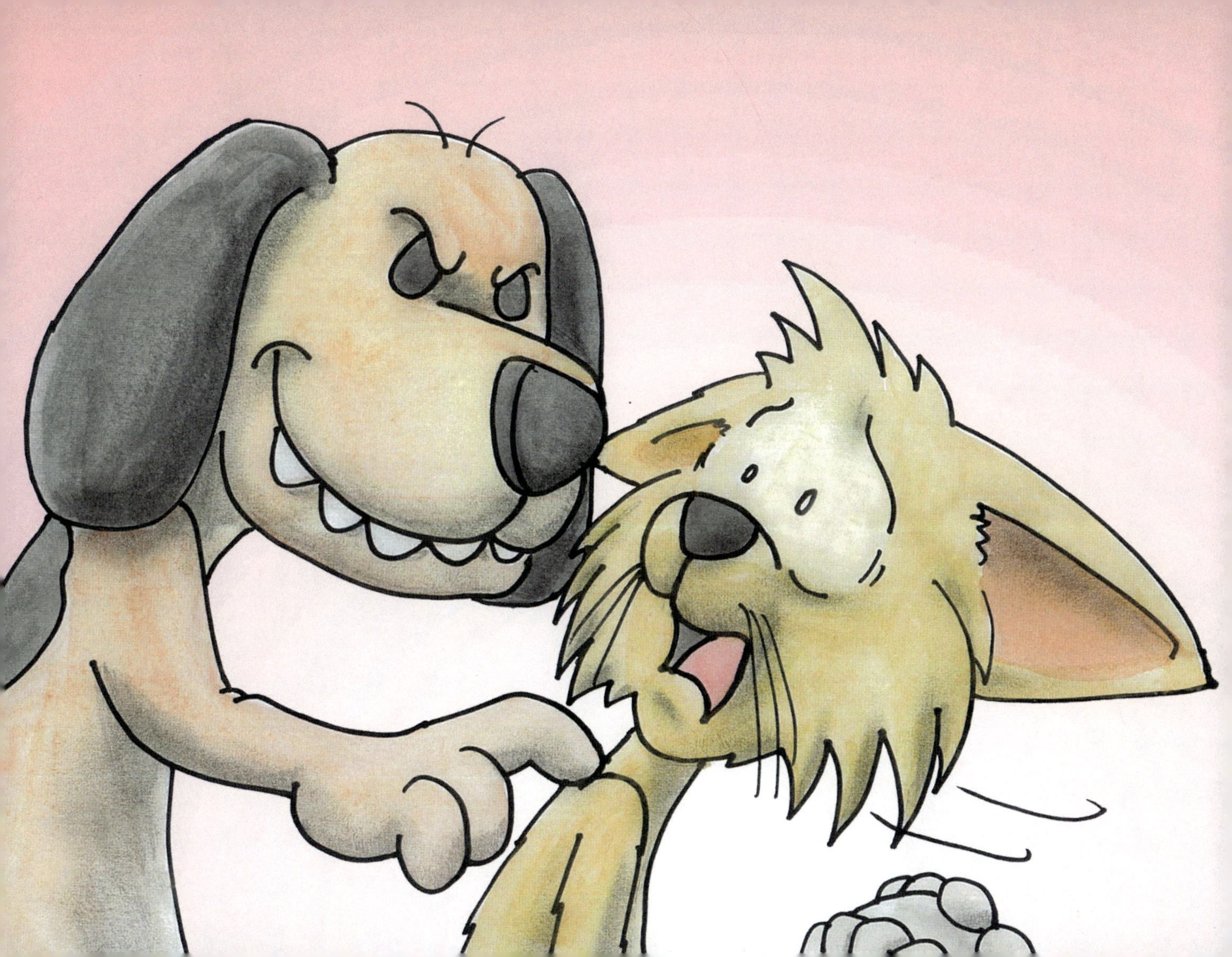

Dog has jam.

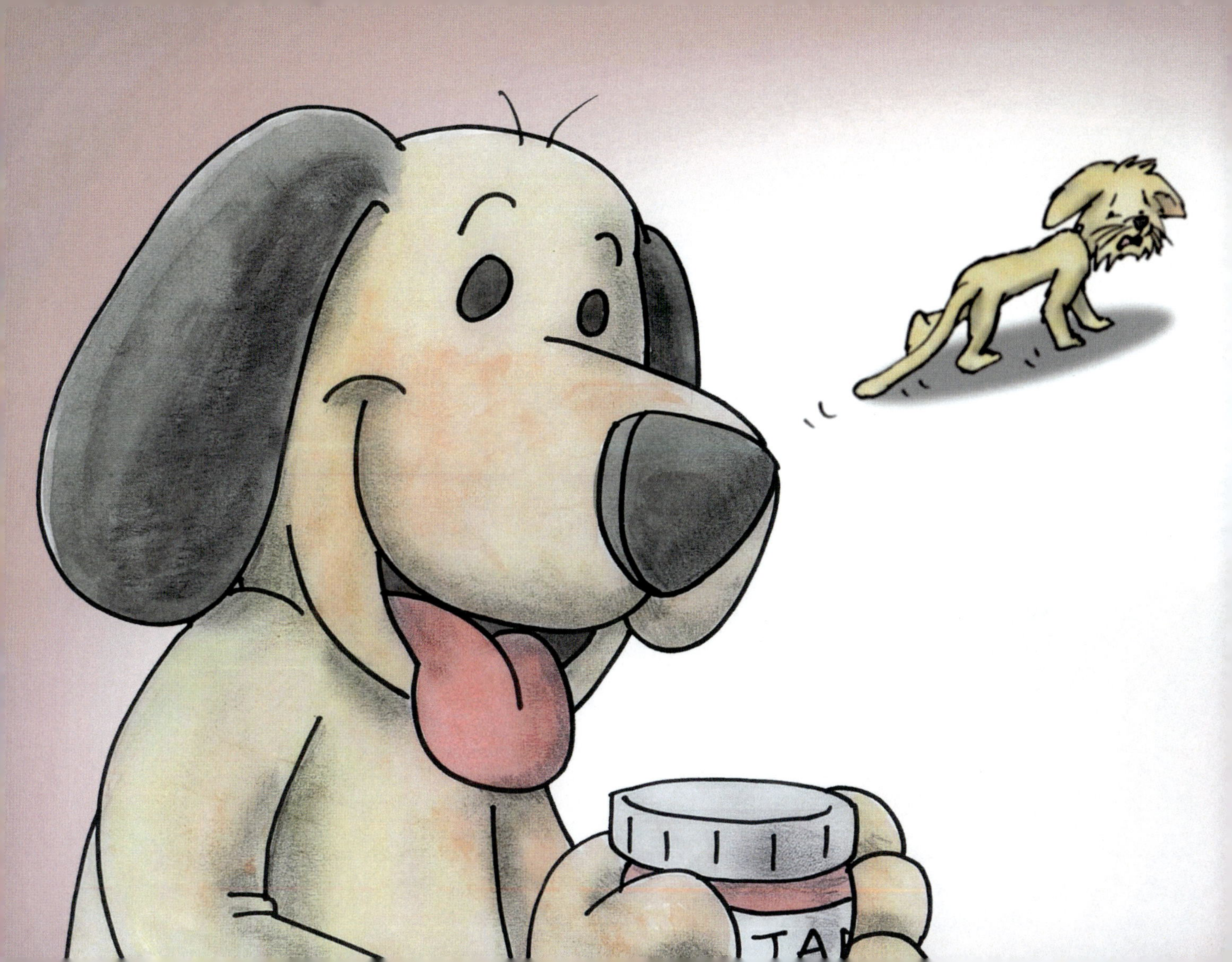

Hog taps Dog.

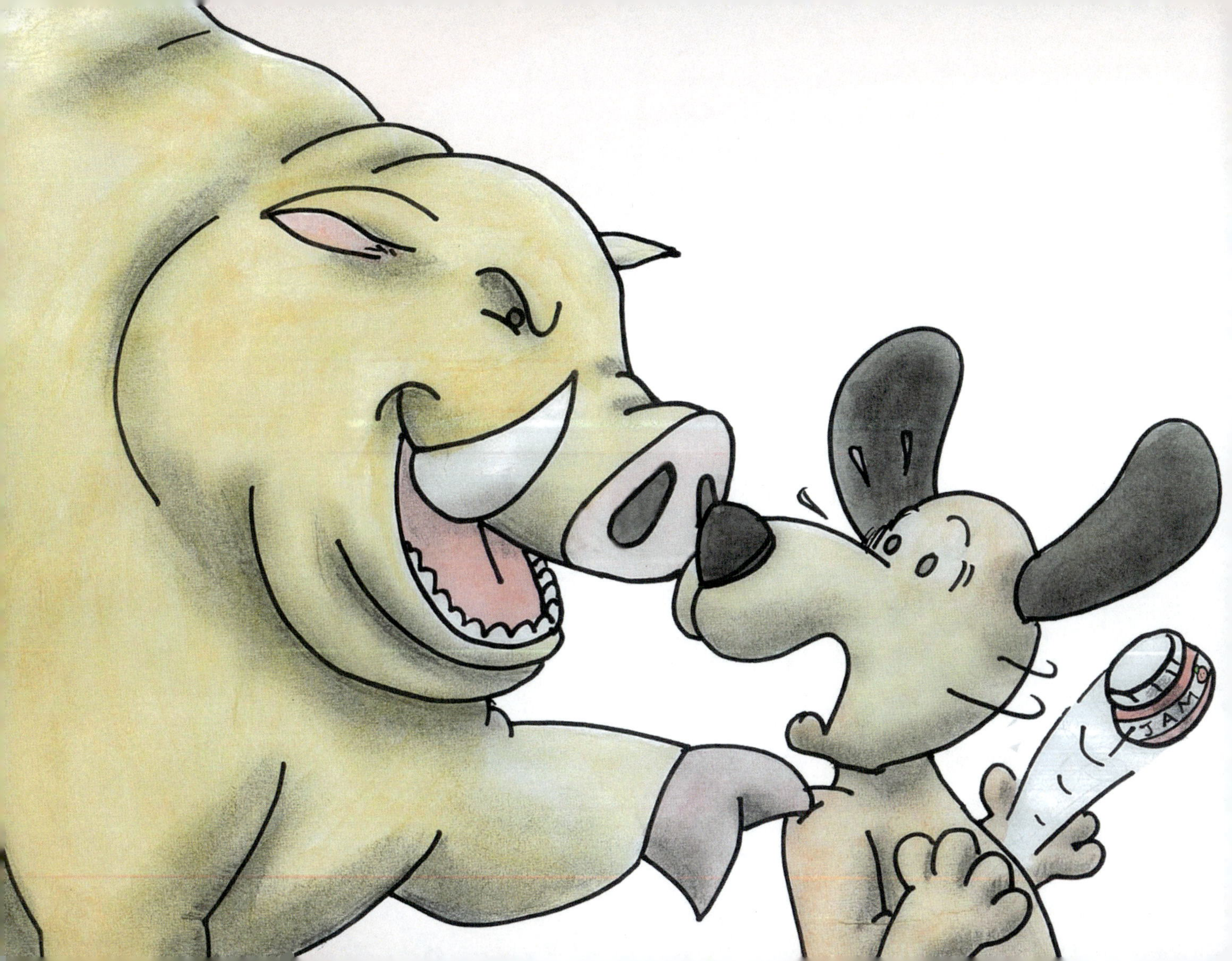
JAM

Lost jam!

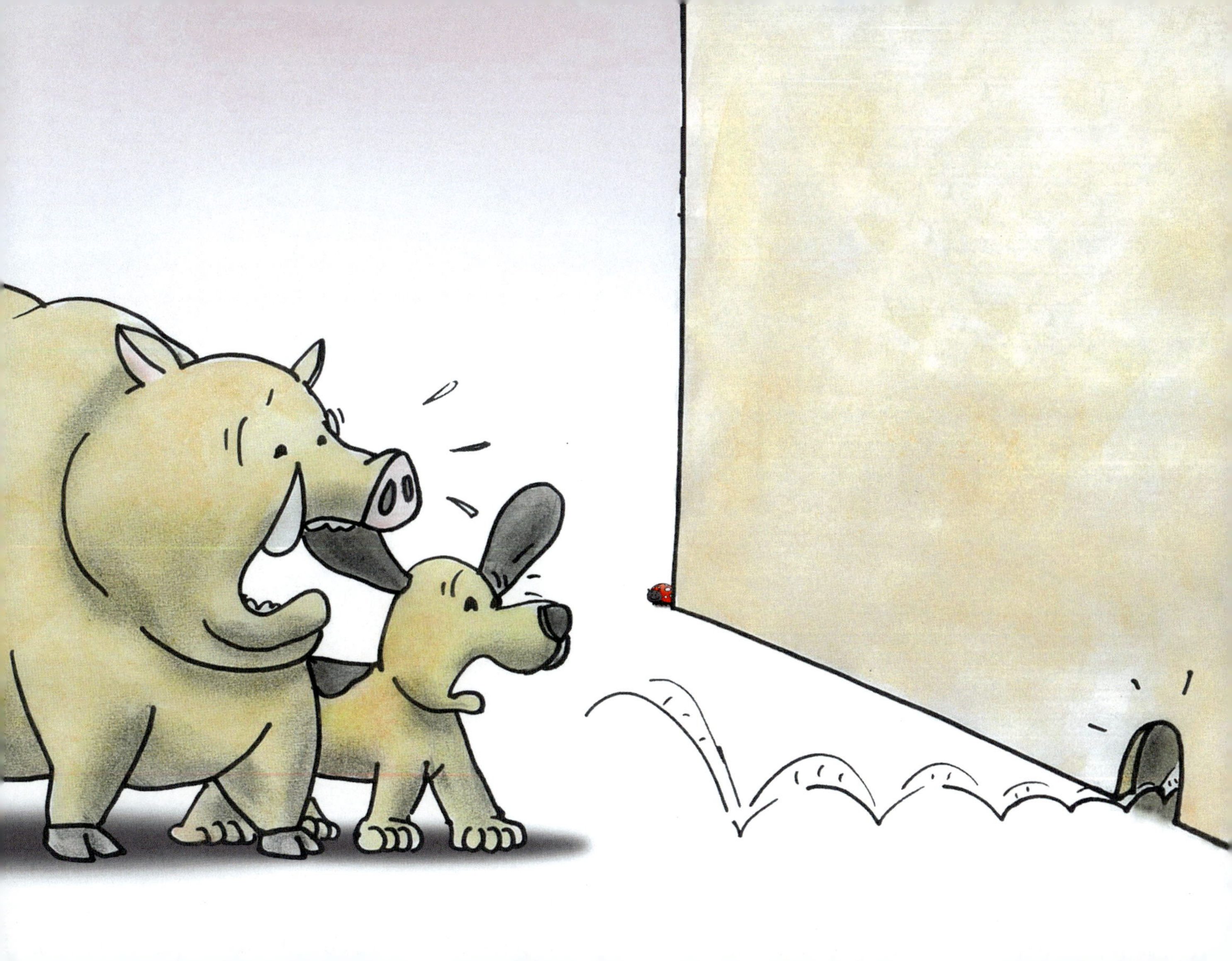

Rat had jam.

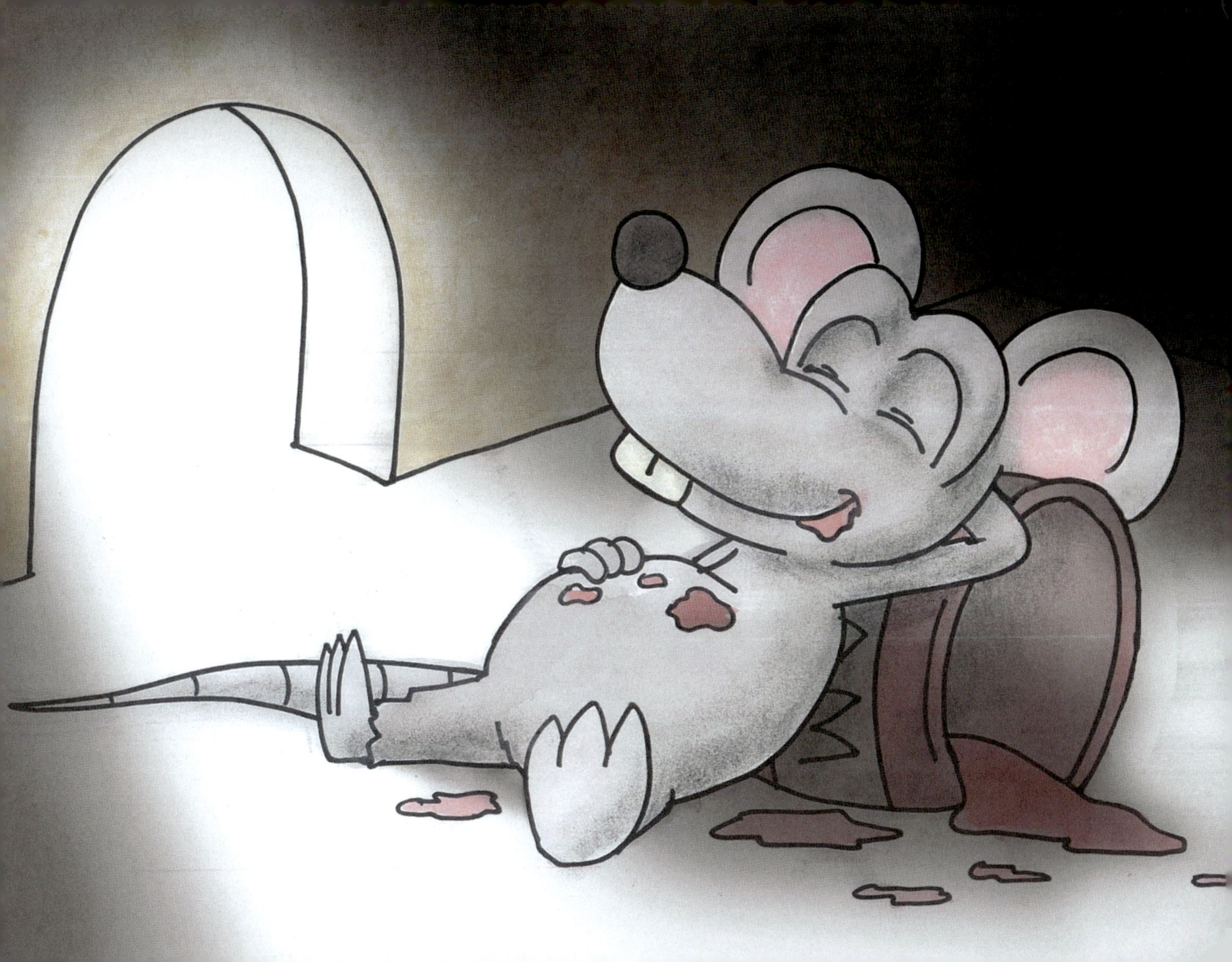

# Reading Guide: Rat and Jam

## Questions for children about the book:

Who had the jam first?    Who was the biggest animal?    Who did you want to get the
Who took the jam from Rat?    Who got the jam last?    jam in the end and why?

Phonic words are words we can read by making the sound of each letter in the word, e.g. m-a-t... mat.

Sight Words are high frequency words that do not follow the rules of phonics. Young children are encouraged to memorize them by sight, e.g. the, a, to, etc.

## Phonics words

rat     hog     taps
bat     and     lost
cat     jam     had
dog     has

## Sight words

This story contains no sight words.

Made in the USA
San Bernardino, CA
26 January 2020